HMS MOST LEAKY

£ 1.95

CONTENTS

STAFFORD PEMBERTON PUBLISHING

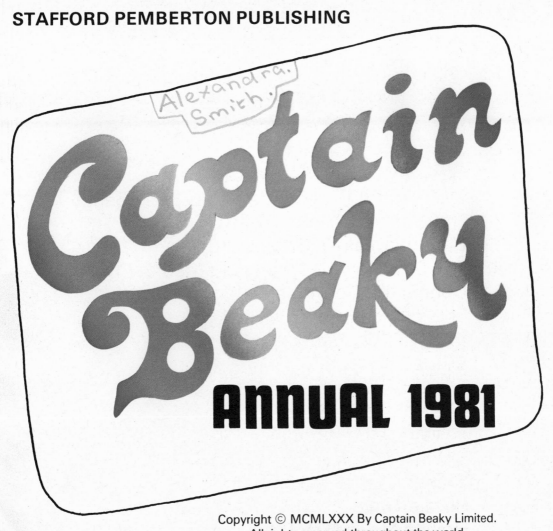

Captain Beaky

ANNUAL 1981

The Making of Captain Beaky

Jeremy Lloyd, the author and originator of the Captain Beaky legend, was himself called Captain Beaky at school, due to his rather long nose — but he didn't mind one bit! All through his life he has written poems about different creatures like Jacques the penniless French mouse, Harold the lonely frog, Desmond the baby duckling and Dilys the Dachshund, not forgetting of course: "The bravest animals in the land — Captain Beaky and his Band; Timid Toad, Reckless Rat, Artful Owl and Batty Bat."

These short poems were scribbled down on the backs of envelopes, film scripts and in letters to friends over a period of twenty years. As he penned them, Jeremy Lloyd never imagined that one day Captain Beaky would be riding high in the top twenty pop charts, or in the best selling list of books as a collection of poems.

Perhaps the road to fame for Captain Beaky and his Band began when Lance Percival read one of Jeremy Lloyd's poems on the radio show 'Start the Week'. Two or three publishers expressed interest, so Jeremy began collecting the poems together. He'd written a few of them years before when working with Keith Michell. Jeremy would write a poem and pass it under the door of Keith Michell's dressing room, and the actor-artist would quickly illustrate it.

Time passed, then one day Jeremy Lloyd met Jonathan Rowlands, a music producer friend, in a coffee bar in the Kings Road. Jeremy showed him some of the poetry he'd written and Jonathan Rowlands suggested they make an LP, putting the poems to music composed by

Jim Parker.

Meanwhile, Keith Michell was appearing on a TV programme with Jim Parker where they each had to talk about their favourite keepsake. Keith brought out one of Jeremy's poems which he read aloud. Jim was amazed and told Keith that he was engaged in making an LP with Jeremy Lloyd, setting the words of that same poem to music. The next day Keith was asked to illustrate the book of poems, to be entitled 'Captain Beaky'.

In 1977 the book of poems appeared, and at the same time the LP of the songs was released, sung and read by stars including Keith Michell, Jeremy Lloyd, Harry Secombe, Peter Sellers and Twiggy.

Polydor brought out the record, and Chappells published the book, but strangely enough, very few copies of either sold. (Perhaps Hissing Sid had a hand in this!)

From left to right: Jeremy Lloyd, Keith Michell, Penelope Keith, Gordon Jackson and Noel Edmonds

Jeremy Lloyd with Anna Neagle on the 'Laugh-In' show

Captain Beaky and his Band looked doomed . . . but then the miracle happened. Noel Edmonds and his radio producer Dave Price heard Captain Beaky on 'Junior Choice'. Both of them liked it so much they borrowed the record from Ed Stewart, and played it on Noel's Sunday morning programme.

Letters began to pour in, sometimes three thousand of them in one week. Someone wrote 'Hissing Sid is Innocent', and more of the Sunday listeners became interested and involved in the Captain Beaky saga.

Polydor put the music back on the market and Chappells decided to re-release the book of poems. The rest is history. Captain Beaky roared into the top five in the pop charts and the book lists and that's how it should be, for: ''The bravest animals in the land are Captain Beaky and his Band. That's Timid Toad, Reckless Rat; Artful Owl and Batty Bat!''

P.S. Hissing Sid is none to pleased — but he's just jealous!

Captain Beaky's Birthday

A late summer's day was drawing to a close and as evening came, black clouds shut out the sun. Later, lightning flashed in the midnight sky. The wind howled. A chorus of oak trees creaked, and rain poured down in torrents.

In one part of the storm-tossed wood was an old oak tree and under a particular branch hung Batty Bat. He was sheltering under a cluster of leaves, trying to count beetles. (Human beings count sheep when they want to sleep — and bats count beetles). After counting four thousand beetles, Batty Bat had managed to sleep for seventeen of the usual forty winks, when a deafening drumroll and cymbal crash of thunder boomed through the wood.

Batty Bat didn't bat an eyelid. But when a gigantic flash of lightning followed, he opened one eye anxiously. "A bat could get electrocuted on a night like this!" squeaked Batty, stretching his skin wings. "Still," he continued philosophically, "I can always drip-dry later."

Batty Bat was just about to start counting beetles again when he heard a distant 'Hoot, Hoot'. "That sounds like Artful Owl," said Batty Bat to himself.

Next moment a wet and bedraggled Owl landed near Batty Bat. "Hello, Artful Owl!" greeted Batty Bat. "How are you?"

"Wet!" sniffed the miserable owl.

"Well, let's hope we get better weather tomorrow," yawned Batty Bat.

"Oh yes. I nearly forgot," said Artful Owl. "It's Captain Beaky's birthday, isn't it?"

"That's right!" squeaked Batty Bat excitedly. "And the whole gang is invited to celebrate it in style. That's why I'm having an early night tonight."

"I think I'll join you," yawned Artful Owl, and so saying he tucked his head under his wing feathers.

The next morning the sun rose big in the sky. After yesterday's downpour the woodland flowers glowed with all the colours of the rainbow and honey bees buzzed busily around them. Swallows zipped through the air, blackbirds sang lilting melodies and sparrows did chirrups by rota.

Captain Beaky was up with the larks as usual, and as it was a special occasion he put on his best yachting cap and gazed at his reflection in the big pool of water which lay near his home. "What Ho!" he cried. "What an absolutely spiffing day for a birthday party!"

Fifteen minutes later he was still preening his tail feathers when Reckless Rat scuttled into view. "Ahoy there, Reckless Rat!" cried the Captain. "Have you got any bright ideas?"

"What kind of bright ideas Cap'n?" asked Reckless Rat.

"Well, you see, I want my birthday to go with a bit of a bang," explained Captain Beaky. "The kind of celebration our gang won't forget in a hurry. So I want some bright ideas on the subject."

"How's about a gun salute?" quipped Reckless Rat.

Captain Beaky tapped his foot on the ground. "M'mm, not a bad idea, Ratty old chap — but I was thinking of something a bit more spectacular, you know?"

Reckless Rat twiddled thoughtfully with his tail. "I could steal into a shop and lasso a few fireworks with my tail," he suggested.

Captain Beaky pondered a moment. "Rockets and Roman candles — do you mean that kind of thing, Ratty?"

"Yes," piped Reckless Rat. "Or we could . . ."

"Whoa! Hang on a minute!" cried the Captain picking up a twig flute with his beak. "I've got an idea. I'll just pipe a note or two on this bosun's whistle here and call the gang together. Then we can pool our ideas."

After playing a few nautical notes on the flute, Captain Beaky and Reckless Rat waited expectantly. First to arrive was Batty Bat, flashing through the air at the speed of a UFO.

Next to appear on the scene was Artful Owl. He looked very tired. "I've been cruising around in the sunlight trying to dry off my feathers," he explained.

Captain Beaky pushed his hat on to the back of his head and scoured the horizon for the final member of the gang. "I wonder where old Timid Toad has got to?" he asked.

"Let's hope he hasn't fallen foul of Hissing Sid the Snake on the way," said Batty Bat.

They waited and waited and Captain Beaky was just about to organise a search party when there was a big 'PLOP' in the centre of the pool nearby and two toady eyes appeared above the surface. Timid Toad swam to the edge of the pool and crawled out beside them.

"How on earth did you get into the pool without us seeing you?" cried Reckless Rat in astonishment.

Timid Toad gave a nervous smile.

"Oh, but I've been in the pool all along", he replied.

Then didn't you hear Captain Beaky's bugle call — I mean, er, flute call?"

"No. Sorry," said Timid Toad. "I was probably submerged too deep to hear it."

"Then what were you doing in the pool?" insisted Rat.

"What does any Toad do in a pool," yawned Artful Owl.

"Actually," said Timid Toad, "I was sitting on the lid of a rusty tin box down there, practising lip reading."

"Practising lip reading! I say!" laughed Captain Beaky. "And whose lips were you reading?"

"Sorry," said Timid Toad. "But I was reading your lips, Captain."

"M'mm. Most interesting!" commented Captain Beaky. "And what do you think I was saying?"

"You were wanting ideas for your birthday party."

"That's it!" cried Captain Beaky gleefully. "I wanted to call you all together to ask for suggestions. You see I wanted my birthday to go with a bit of a fizz. So how about some suggestions, chaps?"

The gang stood around pondering for a moment. "Why not go for a cruise in our ship HMS Most Leaky?" suggested Artful Owl.

"Yes!!" cried Timid Toad excitedly. "And capture Hissing Sid and hang him from the yard-arm."

"No. We'll give Hissing Sid a miss today," said Captain Beaky. "Any other suggestions?"

"Yes," volunteered Batty Bat.

You could tie a piece of string to my legs and fly me as a kite.''

''No, you dear old Bat,'' declined Captain Beaky. ''But thanks for the offer.''

Meanwhile, Reckless Rat was stroking his whiskers and peering into the pool where Timid Toad had surfaced. ''Timid Toad. Did you say something about sitting on the lid of a rusty tin box?'' he asked.

Timid Toad nodded.

''By Jove — do you think there may be something in the box?'' asked Captain Beaky.

''Just a thought, Captain,'' said Reckless Rat modestly.

''Right then! We'll have a Birthday Treasure-Hunt. That's what we'll do!'' declared Captain Beaky.

It was well after midday by the time Captain Beaky and his crew had organised themselves. First they had to bail out their biscuit tin boat *HMS Most Leaky* which was quarter filled with water after the storm. Next, Captain Beaky, Reckless Rat and Batty Bat lifted the winch on board. By operating the winch they hoped to haul the 'treasure chest' on to the deck of *HMS Most Leaky*, then carry their prize home. By the time they were all prepared, Artful Owl was fast asleep on top of the mast, his feathers now dry and warm.

''Wake up, Artful Owl,'' ordered Captain Beaky. ''I want you to be our look-out from now on.''

''Aye, aye, Captain!'' replied the Owl.

''All hands on deck?'' asked Captain Beaky, and seeing that this was so, he called, ''Anchors aweigh! Full sail ahead,'' and the crew danced and cheered as *HMS Most Leaky* drifted out of the reeds in the direction of the middle of the pool.

Little known to Captain Beaky and

his crew, two *very* beady eyes were watching from amidst thick grass on the dark side of the pool. Behind those beady eyes lurked the sneaky sinister mind of Hissing Sid the Snake. His body writhed and twitched as he saw the boat cruise by. "A treasure hunt indeed!" hissed Sid. "Why don't they invite *me* on board? I'll tell you why! They think I'd steal their treasure — that's why. And it would serve them right! Humph! Never a kindly thought for a poor old snake they haven't. And a snake like me could make the owner of a treasure a very good friend. I'm not as slimy as I look you know . . ."

Sid stopped, eyes agleam, because *HMS Most Leaky* was slowing down . . .

On board, Batty Bat was helping to unfurl the sail, and Reckless Rat was getting ready to lower the anchor with his tail. In the water, ahead of the boat, swam Timid Toad, like a mud-coloured porpoise. Suddenly, the Toad stopped.

"Drop the anchor!" yelled the captain. "We've reached the spot. Treasure Ho!" Then, "Right, you merry band. It's time to operate the winch and lower the grappling hook over the side."

Captain Beaky looked around. "Now, Timmy old chap," he called to Toad. But there was no toad to be seen. "Where is that fellow?"

"It's all right, Captain!" reassured Artful Owl. "Timid Toad can understand you. He's down by the treasure — lip reading again."

"Ah, splendid!" enthused Captain Beaky. "You winch down the rope, Ratty and then Timid Toad can swim down and fix the grappling hook on to the treasure chest."

"Aye, aye, Cap'n," piped Reckless Rat, winding down the rope.

Deep in the pool, Timid Toad swam, guiding the hook until it was above the treasure chest. Then he fixed the hook under the handle of the box and swam to the surface and gave the thumbs-up signal to the watching crew.

"Haul away!" bellowed Captain Beaky; and Reckless Rat, assisted by Batty Bat slowly turned the handle of the winch. Captain Beaky lent a willing hand, too, and soon they'd lifted the rusted tin box on board.

Moments later, Timid Toad dragged himself on board and the crew eagerly gathered around the tin box.

"It just looks like a silly old tin box," observed Batty Bat.

"It can't be *that* worthless," squeaked Reckless Rat excitedly, "because it's *locked*!"

"Hang on a jiff," warned Captain Beaky. "There's an old label on the side here. Now what does it say? It says . . . 'BEWARE . . . JACK IN THE BOX!' Well, shiver me timbers! It's an old Jack-in-the-Box that someone has thrown away. It's just as jolly well we didn't open it. It would have given us a nasty old fright and probably sunk the old tub!"

Suddenly from the mast head Artful Owl gave a warning hoot. "Enemy on the port side. Something moved in the grass!"

Batty Bat immediately zipped into the air on a reconnaissance flight and sent back a series of coded squeaks.

"He says it's Hissing Sid!" gasped Timid Toad. "Don't you think it's time we went home. I'm feeling weak with hunger . . ."

"Not to worry!" chuckled Captain Beaky, pulling off the tin's label. "We'll start for home right away. But enroute we'll drop the tin overboard at the edge of the bank where Hissing Sid is lurking!"

Hissing Sid looked at the rusted tin box with greedy beady eyes. "This could be interesting," hissed Sid, trying to prise open the lid. "And it must be something of value because the box is locked. I'll bet the silly Captain Beaky and his daft band of half-wit sailors didn't know how to pick the lock. But that'll be a piece of cake to a sneaky snake like me . . ."

Sid squirmed closer, and using his forked tongue he twisted it into the lock — first one way — then the other . . . Just one more twist then . . . BA-BOOOIINGG! ZOOIIINNG! The horrible-faced Jack-in-the-Box shot out of the tin and frightened the living daylights out of poor Sid. His beady eyes nearly popped out of his head and he twisted himself up like a corkscrew with fright.

"What the 'eck happened?" gasped Sid.

Captain Beaky and his merry band saw it all and they couldn't stop laughing! "It's the funniest thing I've seen for years!" chuckled the Captain. "The best birthday present I could have wished for. So now we'll just turn for home, sail into the setting sun and sing a few sea songs on the way. That'll cap an absolutely spiffing day, or my name's not Captain Beaky and you're not the best crew that ever sailed the seven seas!"

How To Make HMS Most Leaky

You can make yourself a model of Captain Beaky's boat *HMS Most Leaky*, if you have an old biscuit tin, some cotton, some coloured paper for sail, plasticine and a thin stick about 450 cm. long for the mast.

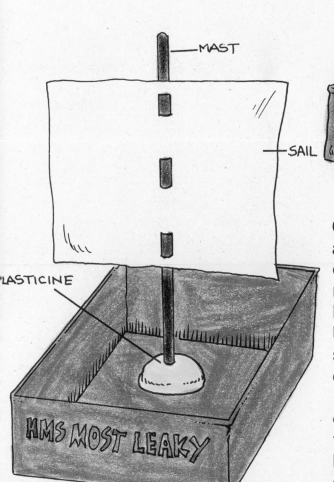

MAST

SAIL

PLASTICINE

HMS MOST LEAKY

BISCUIT TIN

Get a thick lump of plasticine and stick it firmly to the centre of the biscuit tin and secure the mast in this. Next, cut two small holes near the centre top and bottom edges of the paper square sail and tie it to the mast with the cotton. Fix with plasticine a label marked *HMS Most Leaky* on the side of the tin. Then, for fun, try to design some cardboard figures of Captain Beaky and his Band (you could try tracing some of the artwork in this book) paint them in water colours and fix them in different places on the boat with plasticine.

SIDS

AND

LADDERS

The game requires two or more players. You will also need a dice and shaker. Each player must throw a six to start. When landing at the bottom of a ladder, move to the top but when landing on Hissing Sid's square, you must go down. Players must score the exact number to finish when they land on number 94 or higher.

Captain Beaky's Dream Cruise

ONE DAY IN THE WOODS CAPTAIN BEAKY WAS DOZING IN HIS HAMMOCK.

CAPTAIN BEAKY WAS ON HIS DREAM CRUISE!

TIMID TOAD WAS IN HIS OWN PRIVATE SWIMMING POOL!

RECKLESS RAT WAS CURLED UP WITH A GIGANTIC LASSOO UNDERNEATH HIM.

18

BATTY BAT AND ARTFUL OWL WERE HAVING A SNOOZE TOGETHER WITH THE REST OF THE BRAVE BAND.

"THIS IS THE LIFE" SAID BEAKY "WE ARE ALL HERE AND NO HISSING SID TO WORRY ABOUT FOR A CHANGE!"

BUT AT THAT VERY MOMENT ON THE PORT SIDE...

"BY JOVE A SUBMARINE" SAID BEAKY "AND ITS GUNS ARE POINTING STRAIGHT AT US!"

SUBMARINE HISSING SID FIRED A DEADLY TORPEDO.

"OH! OH! THIS IS A NIGHTMARE, A TERRIBLE, TERRIBLE, NIGHTMARE!" CRIED TIMID TOAD.

"YOU'RE RIGHT!" SAID CAPTAIN BEAKY "IT IS A NIGHTMARE! AND IF I DON'T WAKE UP PRETTY QUICKLY, WE'LL ALL BE SUNK."

"PHEW! I WOKE UP JUST IN TIME, BUT AT LEAST WE FOOLED HISSING SID AGAIN!".

More About The Making of Captain Beaky

Jeremy Lloyd, the creator of Captain Beaky, was born in London. His mother was a Tiller girl and his father an army Colonel, who wanted his son to take up a military career. But thankfully for us, Jeremy was more drawn to the artistic and creative side of life.

At the age of twelve he left school and went to live with his grandparents at a home for retired gentle folk. There he read lots of books and engaged in many fascinating conversations with the old folk which taught him a lot. He later studied sculpture for three years then became a Management Trainee at Simpsons store in Piccadilly. There he had some amusing experiences, which he put to good use when it came to writing scripts for the top comedy programme he created **Are You Being Served?**

After leaving Simpsons he became, in his own words, "one of the best light-bulb inspectors ever employed." This involved peering through a magnifying glass at light-bulbs and throwing them down a shaft if they were faulty.

He then acquired a job as a Scientific Advisor with an industrial paint firm. During this time he saw a badly-scripted film at the local cinema and decided he could do better. He set to and wrote a script in an old school-

Jeremy Lloyd

report book and sent it to Earl St. John, then head of Pinewood Studios. This story (about the Loch Ness Monster) was accepted and made into the film called **What a Whopper** starring Adam Faith.

Jeremy Lloyd's literary career had begun. During the making of **What a Whopper** he met Jon Pertwee and this meeting resulted in Jeremy writing scripts for **6.5 Special** — a popular music programme of the late fifties. Other scriptwriting jobs came his way, and he also began to develop his acting talents in such films as **Those Magnificent Men in their Flying Machines** and **Man in the Moon.**

After a shooting accident during

Keith Michell

the filming of **The Wrong Box,** Jeremy spent his convalescence time writing poems which were later to be used in the Captain Beaky collection.

A comedy novel, **The Further Adventures of Captain Gregory Dangerfield** followed, and this was published by Michael Joseph. Then came the comedy series **Are You Being Served,** after which he met up with an old pal, Lance Percival. Together they thought up the 'Whodunnit' detective series panel game, which was very successful.

Jeremy Lloyd's hobbies include driving old cars. He lives in a cottage near St James's Palace, and is "amazed, astonished and absolutely delighted" by the success of Captain Beaky.

KEITH MICHELL

Keith Michell is the illustrator of the Captain Beaky book of poems published by Chappell and Co. Ltd, but he is probably better known as the narrator and singer of the Captain Beaky hit singles and LP.

Keith was born in Adelaide, Australia and when he was old enough he trained as an art teacher there, eventually teaching art for two years. Although probably better known as an actor, Keith Michell thinks of himself primarily as an artist.

His acting career began when he gained admission to London's Old Vic Theatre School and he later toured with the Young Vic Company. He was specially chosen to play the part of Charles II in a musical, and this was to be his debut performance in London's West End.

He travelled back to his homeland in 1953 with the Stratford Memorial Theatre Company, then returned in 1955 to Shakespeare country — Stratford — to play leading roles in many of the Shakespeare plays and also a number of films which included **Gypsy and the Gentleman** with Melina Mercouri. As a welcome break from the pressures of acting, Keith managed to sail to Jamaica on a slow banana boat and painted enough pictures for a one man show at the Whibley Galleries, London. At a later date he exhibited a second set of paintings there.

More films, stage-plays, shows and television drama productions followed and Keith is probably best known for his role as Henry VIII in the television series **The Six Wives of Henry VIII.**

Keith's meeting with Jeremy Lloyd has already been described and since illustrating the Captain Beaky book Keith was made Artistic Director of the Chichester Festival Theatre where he combined his acting and illustrative talents by designing the sets for **Twelfth Night** and also directing the play.

Keith Michell, artist and actor, is married and has a son and a daughter. It's a good bet that they're all Captain Beaky fans too!

How To Make Hissing Sid

To make a toy Hissing Sid
You will need:
A long piece of string. Ten or more empty cotton reels. Two corks. An old rubber ball. Red felt. Green, Red and Black paint. Paint the reels and ball green. Then paint red diamonds on each reel. Paint the corks black. Knot string and thread through one cork — then through each cotton reel, finally through ball and second cork. Stick red felt tongue to Hissing Sid's face.

This makes a good pull-along toy as well as being a colourful ornament for your room.

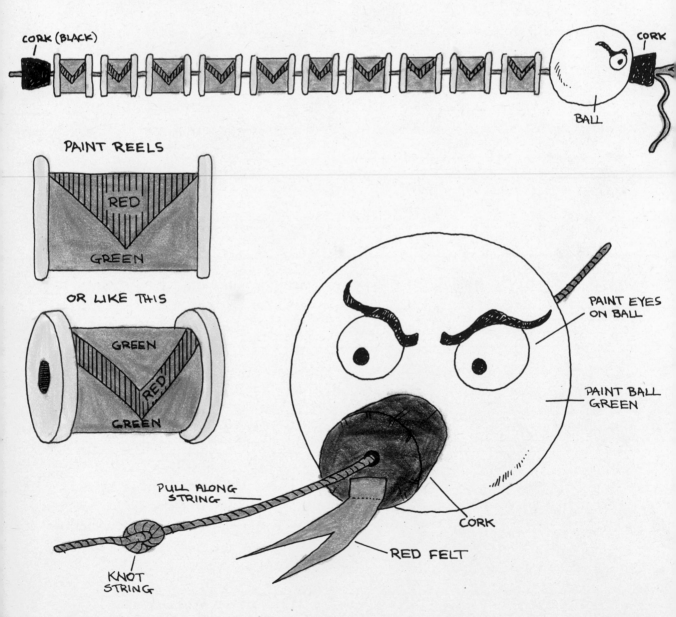

CORK (BLACK) CORK

BALL

PAINT REELS

RED
GREEN

OR LIKE THIS

GREEN
RED
GREEN

PAINT EYES ON BALL

PAINT BALL GREEN

CORK

PULL ALONG STRING

RED FELT

KNOT STRING

Captain Beaky's Crossword

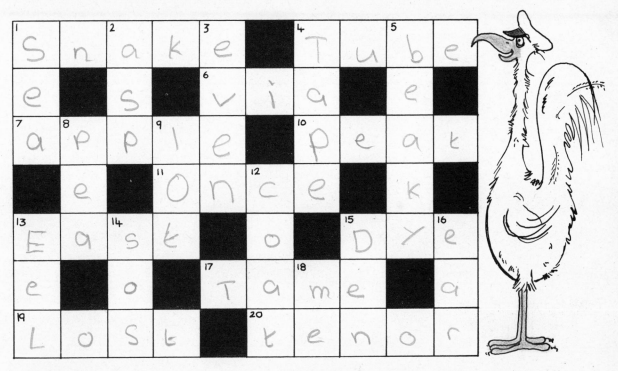

ACROSS:
1. Hissing Sid
4. Holds toothpaste
6. By way of; or through
7. Fruit
10. Fuel (from bog)
11. One time only
13. Opposite of west
15. Change colour
17. Not wild
19. Mislaid
20. Male singer

DOWN:
1. Ocean
2. Another 'Sid'
3. Three is odd, four is ...?
4. ... Measure
5. Captain ...
8. Tiny green vegetable
9. More than a little
12. You wear it in cold weather
13. Wriggly fish
14. Distress call
15. Wild beast's lair
16. You have one on each side of your head
18. Myself

Answers to Crossword:

DOWN
1. Sea 2. Asp 3. Even 4. Tape 5. Beaky 8. Pea 9. Lot 12. Coat 13. Eel 14. SOS 15. Den 16. Ear. 18. Me

ACROSS
1. Snake 4. Tube 6. Via 7. Apple 10. Peat 11. Once 13. East 15. Dye 17. Tame 19. Lost 20. Tenor

25

The Day Blanche Nearly Learned To Fly

Baby owls, like most baby birds, do not fly the minute they are born. It takes a while for their feathers to grow, and it takes time for them to grow strong enough to be able to practice flying.

Blanche, the baby owl, was four weeks old. She was born in a warm comfortable nest in the corner of a barn. The barn had been her only world for those first four weeks. She knew it inside out, left to right, and top to bottom. In fact she knew it so well that she was becoming restless and eager to go out and see the big world outside.

What else was there to do, except eat, sleep and study the barn? What else was there to do when Mother Owl left the nest to find food? Well, I'll tell you. There were plenty of ideas going round in Blanche's head. She began to want to fly out of the barn door. She wanted to see the big green field and the chickens and the horses. She wanted to fly out to the big pond and see the swans. In fact, she was longing to see all the things that her mother had told her about.

One sunny morning just after breakfast, when Mother Owl was away, Blanche decided to practice her numbers. She had taught herself to count up to ten, with her mother's help of course! It had taken a good week or so, but now she could do it with her big eyes closed.

"Er, one . . . two . . . three . . . four . . ." and so on. She counted until she had reached ten. Suddenly she jumped up. "If I can count up to ten, then I *MUST* be able to fly!" she said loudly. I'm not sure just how Blanche had come to this conclusion, but she seemed quite certain that this was the case.

She looked at the bale of straw outside her nest, and then looked down at her feet. Suddenly, with one hop, she found herself sitting on the bale of straw. She laughed loudly, "I did it!"

With one more hop, she was on the barn floor. Then, step by step, she walked towards the barn door. "One, two, three, four, five, six, seven, eight, nine, ten," she counted to herself over and over again.

Outside the barn door the sun shone brightly and she ruffled her wispy feathers with glee. On to the green grass she hopped, gazing up at the blue sky. "Soon *I* shall be up there!" she said to herself.

On she hopped until she came to a large branch. It lay in the grass surrounded by yellow primroses. "This will do, I shall jump from *this* branch," she said.

So on she climbed, clasping her two feet around the bark. Then, leaning her head back and looking up into the blue sky, she shouted out as loud as she possibly could, "One...two...three...four..." and so on until she reached ten.

The trouble was, she had to start all over again because she realised just in time that seven does not come after five, six should fit in there somewhere! She only just stopped herself from jumping. "Oh dear, I *must* get it right," she said, "there is no point in flying if I can't even count up to ten properly."

On reaching ten all the way without a mistake, she took a deep breath and jumped up into the air as high as she possibly could.

Plonk! Oh dear, poor Blanche! There she lay, flat on her tummy. Her left leg was crossed over her right. Her beak had stuck into a tuft of grass and there was a primrose tickling her nose. She was quite in a daze. Blanche opened her beak and howled.

"My, my, it is a good thing that I chose a branch on the ground. If it had been any higher, I might have really hurt myself! Oh dear, will I never, ever be able to fly?" she howled again.

Up she hopped and ruffled her wispy feathers and sadly began to head back to the barn. At that moment she tripped on a rather large toadstool, and yet again fell flat on her beak. "Oh, I wish I never was an owl! Owls are meant to fly and I can't. In fact, I can't even walk properly! Why wasn't I born a horse, or a dog, or a duck, or something like that?" she screamed loudly.

Her crying reached the ears of the swans on the pond, and they all turned their heads. The horses in the field stopped eating and turned towards the howling sound. Last but not least, Mother Owl in the barn flew over quickly when she heard the crying.

"Whatever is that noise?" said Mother Owl as she flew past the horses. There in the primroses she found poor Blanche flat on her tummy and sobbing loudly. "Oh my dear!" she said, "I wondered where you had got to!"

"Oh Mother, I can't fly. I'm useless at being an owl! Owls fly, but I can't! Whatever is going to happen to me?" sobbed Blanche.

Mother Owl helped her up from the ground and sat her on her knee. She placed her large, comforting wing around Blanche and said, "My little one, before you can fly, and you will, there are certain things which must come first. Now listen, Blanche dear. Firstly your feathers must grow. You need strong feathers to catch the wind. Look at yours, they are still wispy, they haven't grown enough. Secondly, you must practice. We will come out here every day, and I will teach you how to fly when you are ready."

So Blanche, feeling reassured by her mother's words, managed to smile. "I *did* want to see the horses and the swans so much, Mother," she said.

Just then, who should be standing behind them but two of the swans from the pond and one of the big brown horses from the field. "Hello, Blanche, it's very nice to meet you!" they said.

A Dormouse is a sort of mouse and a sort of squirrel and as you know, squirrels like to sleep a lot during the winter. Dennis the Dormouse did too.

One thing he hated was to be woken up during his deep deep sleep; and the trouble was — the SLIGHTEST noise would waken him. A noisy radio; a car horn honking, someone slamming a door, or a crow cawing.

Dennis tried making himself some earplugs out of tiny acorns, but every time he dropped off to sleep, the acorns would drop out with a ''plop'' and disturb him again.

Then little Dennis found a remedy. He dug a deep hole in the ground, furnished it with food and then when it snowed, the white fluffy blanket that formed above him kept the warmth in — and the noise *out!*

The Music of Captain Beaky

THE RECIPE FOR SUCCESS:

Here is the recipe for the Captain Beaky music success: mix together the poems of Jeremy Lloyd and the music of Jim Parker; add the combined talents of Keith Michell, Harry Secombe, Twiggy and Peter Sellers and take them all to the Olympic Studios in London, where producer Hugh Murphy is waiting to record them.

For your main course — listen to Keith Michell, Jeremy Lloyd, Harry Secombe, Peter Sellers and Twiggy singing about the secret lives of Desmond the Duck, Herbert the Hedgehog or Harold the Frog. And if the sound of such delicious music whets your appetite you're ready to give the Captain Beaky singles a try.

For refreshments — try singing along yourself to the music of the Captain Beaky Band.

Hugh Murphy, Twiggy and Jeremy Lloyd

JIM PARKER — Composer of the Captain Beaky Music

Jim Parker, who composed the music for the Captain Beaky Album and singles, learnt to play the oboe in the band of the Dragoon Guards. Later he studied at the Guildhall School of Music before joining the City of Birmingham Symphony Orchestra. After this he came to London as a freelance player.

Before writing the Captain Beaky music he wrote the theme music for the TV Series **Village Hall,** and with Wally K. Daly he wrote the musicals **Follow the Star** and **Make me a World.** Jim is also a member of the Barrow Poets and has recorded much of his music with them.

JONATHAN ROWLANDS — The man who helped make Captain Beaky a Success

Jonathan Rowlands was one of the leading lights in getting the Captain Beaky music into production. With his partner Hugh Murphy he had produced Sir John Betjeman's albums and when he met Jeremy Lloyd by chance in a Kings Road coffee bar, he gave Jeremy a copy of the Sir John Betjeman album **Banana Blush.** Jeremy Lloyd was enchanted by Jim Parker's music, to which Sir John's poems were read, and this sparked off the Jim Parker-Jeremy Lloyd partnership.

Jonathan Rowlands was just the man to get the idea off the ground as he is an experienced manager and organiser, having been associated with the guitarist Jeff Beck and the singers Tom Jones, Rod Stewart and Englebert Humperdinck.

THE CAPTAIN BEAKY ALBUM

For the Captain Beaky LP each of the artists; Jeremy Lloyd, Keith Michell, Peter Sellers, Twiggy and Harry Secombe have added their own ideas to the written poems. The results are often original and always exciting. The words are sometimes spoken, and at other times sung. Now and again these two ways of presentation are combined.

When the LP was originally made, there were two ways of recording the material. The first was to record the artist in a studio with a full orchestra, and by using this method the song was completed in one session. The other, more complex method of recording was to record one of the artists, accompanied by Jim Parker on piano. Later, by stages, different sections of the orchestra were added to the track. This is a difficult process which requires great skill in recording technique.

On the Captain Beaky Album both methods of recording were used in an effort to give the listener the best sound quality.

Twiggy

TWIGGY, HARRY SECOMBE & PETER SELLERS

Apart from Keith Michell and Jeremy Lloyd, the three other artists who sing on the Captain Beaky Album are Twiggy, Harry Secombe and Peter Sellers.

Twiggy is probably the most famous model in recent years. Her first big acting break came in **The Boyfriend.** Since then she has appeared on many TV shows and has recorded two albums apart from the Captain Beaky album.

Harry Secombe is well known both as a singer and comedian. He has appeared in countless film and stage plays and is well liked both on and off the stage. In 1963 he was awarded the CBE for his services to charity and in the early 70s broke into the literary scene with his first novel called **Twice Brightly,** which was a best seller. Probably his most famous radio series was the **Goon Show** when he starred with Michael Bentine, Spike Milligan and, of course Peter

Harry Secombe

Peter Sellers

Sellers — the other star on the Captain Beaky album.

The late Peter Sellers was one of the greatest comedians in show business, with many screen portraits to his name. Perhaps his most famous was his role as the bumbling French detective Inspector Clouseau in **The Pink Panther.** Peter usually had his audiences splitting their sides with laughter. Even his co-actors couldn't keep their faces straight! Because of this the director Blake Edwards, was forced to cut so many hilarious sequences out of the films that he decided to string them all together again at a later date and show the 'series of cuts' as a short comedy film in its own right.

Twiggy and Harry Secombe are household names, and along with Jeremy Lloyd and Keith Michell, they are now even more famous for their splendid association with Captain Beaky. Even Hissing Sid wouldn't begrudge them such a well-earned success.

Dilys the Dachshund

Dilys the Dachshund was just an ordinary dachshund. You know, the type of dog that has a long, long body and short little legs. Dilys lived an ordinary dachshund kind of life, going about her ordinary dachshund business — just like any ordinary dachshund.

Then one day it began to snow, and Dilys, with such short little legs found it awfully difficult to walk through the snow. So she walked on her back legs — on tiptoes.

A talent spotter saw her and offered her a job as a ballerina. Fame came overnight to Dilys at the ballet when a prince in the royal box applauded her skill.

And from that day on, whenever it snows, dachshunds all over the world think of Dilys the Dachshund. But unfortunately — most of these dachshunds find it difficult to find ballet shoes to fit their tiny doggy feet.

37

Stitch Them Up!

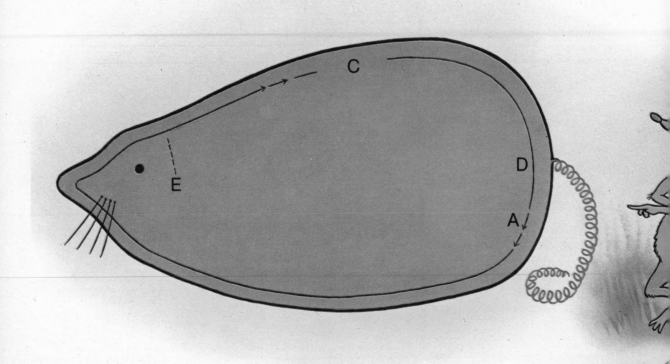

How to make Reckless Rat:

From fur fabric or similar material, cut two body pieces. Place furry sides together (facing each other), and stitch firmly from A to C.

   Turn furry side out and stuff with kapok or similar material. Close C-D by ladder stitch. Cut *two pairs* of ears. Stitch with furry sides together.   Then stitch to body at E.   Attach plaited string tail at D, making loop for lasso. A small circle of black felt makes the eyes. Make whiskers by stitching lengths of cotton where shown on both sides of face. These can be stiffened with clear nail varnish for realistic effect.

   You can add a paper "stetson" hat to make Reckless Rat complete.

How to make a toy Toad:

Cut out two pieces in green felt. On one piece sew or stick some shapes in darker green or brown for 'warts'. Stitch firmly together, leaving opening for filling. Stitch across leg pieces where shown, then fill two-thirds full with rice or lentils. Sew together completely.

Stick on two black circles, and two white circles for eyes as in diagram.

Timid Toad Goes Missing

In the woodland where Captain Beaky and his Band lived, there was always some good deed that needed doing. The Band enjoyed doing good deeds — it was what they did best. Quite often they would make up songs about their adventures and sing them around the camp fire at night. This meant they were always singing, because they were forever doing good deeds!

One day it came to pass that Hissing Sid, an awful, evil snake, had done one bad thing too many. Why was he *so* evil, you might ask! Well, he delighted in biting people's feet, or arms, or legs whenever he got the chance. He thought it was great fun! The woodland folk who lived in the area were more than frightened, they could not sleep in peace because of Hissing Sid and his dreadful deeds.

Something certainly had to be done, so Captain Beaky called his Band together to decide on a plan.

"One of us must be the bait, and the rest of us can hide and be ready for the right moment to jump!" said Artful Owl. "I'll be the one, of course," he added bravely.

"Oh no, I'll be the one!" said Reckless Rat. "Let me lasso him with my tail!"

Poor Timid Toad readily agreed to this. "Of course, we'll come to help you as soon as Hissing Sid gives in," he said to Reckless Rat.

"No, no, *I'll* fly up into a tree and drop a rock on his head!" said Batty Bat bravely. Batty Bat certainly lived up to his name.

"However will you lift a rock off the ground?" laughed Artful Owl.

"H'mmm," said Batty Bat, scratching his head. "I hadn't thought of it that way." He blushed in embarrassment.

"No, hold on everyone," said Artful Owl, "there's only one of us that Hissing Sid will bother to attack. The rest of us will have to lie in wait."

"Good, good," said Timid Toad, wiping the sweat from his forehead and heaving a loud sigh of relief.

His sigh of relief came *too* soon! Artful Owl patted him on the back and said, "Brave Toad, *you're* the one! Hissing Sid will find you a most tasty meal. He just can't resist Toad on toast!"

Before Timid Toad could even shriek in fright he was pushed off into the darkness. "Good luck, brave Toad!" the others said, and poor Toad had to hop off, his eyes nearly popping out of his head with fright.

Captain Beaky, Artful Owl and Reckless Rat followed shortly behind him, while Batty Bat flew on ahead above the trees. Suddenly Captain Beaky stopped dead in his tracks. The others had not seen him stop, and each in turn bumped into him.

Bump! Bump! OUCH!

"Sch, sch!" whispered Captain Beaky, "Batty Bat is sending a message." (I must explain to you, in case you didn't know, that bats can send sound waves through the air. This can be a great help in dangerous times like these!)

The message read that the evil Hissing Sid had captured Timid Toad. With this terrible news, the Band began to run, guided carefully in the right direction by clever Batty Bat and his sound waves. They ran as fast as they could to Hissing Sid's lair, a small, but comfortable, leafy hide-away.

"I'll get a pole," said Reckless Rat, trying not to sound hysterical. "I'll stop him getting back into his lair."

Just then Hissing Sid came rolling and jumping along — quite an unusual thing for a snake to be doing. He went right past his lair, making no attempt to get in. In fact, he leaped right past Captain Beaky and his Band and disappeared into the night.

Startled and confused, Captain Beaky and his Band followed, in hot pursuit.

"Did you see that?" shrieked Reckless Rat, running as fast as his legs would carry him. They found Hissing Sid absolutely exhausted and quite dizzy, he was leaning against a log, panting.

"Timid Toad is inside Hissing Sid!" called out Batty Bat, landing on the ground. "I can see the lump. Pull him out quickly!"

The gang set to and soon had Timid Toad free.

"Where is he?" asked Timid

Toad, breathing the cool night air again. "What's happened? You see, I was so frightened and felt quite ill, so I jumped into a hollow stick and hid!

Poor Toad was *most* confused.

Hissing Sid slunk gratefully away. He was mighty relieved to be rid of such a wriggling lump.

By now, Timid Toad was feeling SO brave, he even took a bow, while the others applauded!

"I don't think that we will be seeing the evil Hissing Sid again," said Captain Beaky. "Come on, let's go and tell the woodland folk the good news!"

Off they marched down the road, patting Timid Toad on the back and shaking his hand.

So, here ends the tale of the bravest Band in all the land. Don't you agree, it is Captain Beaky and his Band?

CHASING HISSING SID

Who captures Sid first? Or does he escape? Each player (up to 5 players) chooses which of the gang they'd like to play for. Using counters to mark the place of each player, take turns to throw the dice. But note that only Nos. 1, 2 and 3 on the dice count. Nos 4, 5 and 6 means you stay where you are until your next throw.

The first to reach Sid wins the game. But remember, if you land on the SID ESCAPES square — you are out of the game!

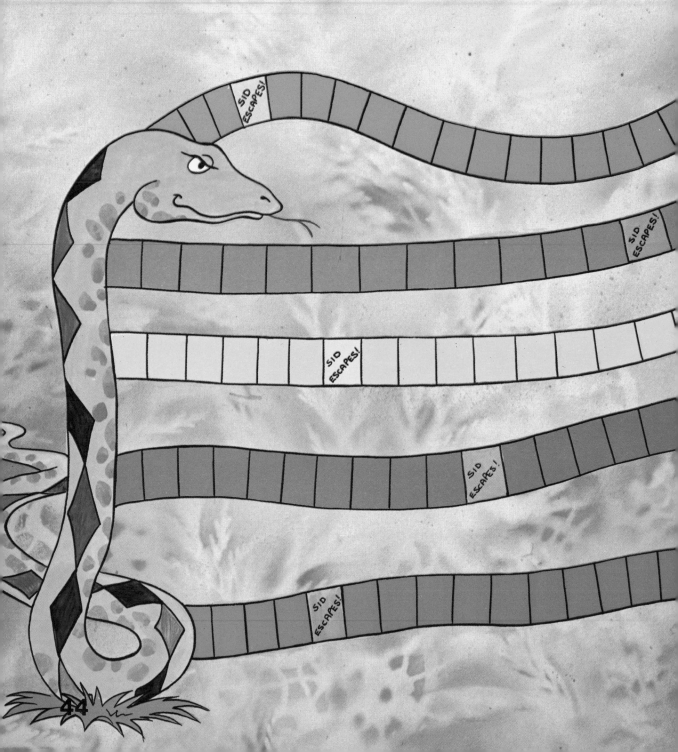

A Walk In The Woods

If you were to take a stroll in a wood on a warm summer's day, what would you see and hear? Perhaps you'd see silver birch trees with their silver-grey bark; oak trees covered with young acorns or beech trees with smooth grey trunks and green oval leaves.

Perched in the branches above your head you might spot a wood-pigeon — a big bird with a white collar of feathers on its neck and hear its song, a gentle coo-cooing. If you are very quiet you might hear the friendly buzzing of the honey bee. Did you know that, by flying, a bee breaks the laws of 'aerodynamics' because (in theory at least) it is supposed to be too heavy to fly with such small wings. So every time you see a bee you are in effect seeing a miracle.

As you walk in the woods think of how the trees looked in the Winter — when their branches were bare; the grass was withered, and there was not a wild flower to brighten the gloom. And yet at the birth of Spring everything is reborn, heralded by the tiny snowdrop flowers pushing up through bleak frosts towards the pale light of the sun.

When you're in a wood, sit down against the trunk of a tree on the edge of the wood and look up. You are bound to see a skylark pouring down a continuous chain of melody as it hovers over its nest in the coarse grass. Watch for acrobatic bluetits and listen for the rhapsodies of the blackbirds and thrushes.

When you're sitting by your favourite tree watch out for your favourite Captain Beaky characters. Some of them are described here.

What kind of snake is Hissing Sid? Is he a GRASS SNAKE?

Did you know that snakes have no breast bones or collar bones and their ribs are not joined, so that when they eat a big meal their ribs flatten out to allow more space. The bones in their head are so loosely set so that the mouth can open to a space three times that of the snake's head! You could then justly accuse Hissing Sid of being swell-headed.

The Grass Snake is the largest of British snakes and just behind the head are two patches of yellow or orange by which it can be identified easily. The Grass Snake is harmless.

Is Batty Bat a PIPISTRELLE BAT?

Bats can twist and turn in the air, and zip around corners even better than birds can. They avoid flying into obstacles by emitting ultra-sonic squeaks which bounce back off solid objects and warn the Bat to avoid them. The head and body of a Pipistrelle measures about 35mm but its wing span is over 20cm. You might see it flying about one night so don't forget to say 'Hello, Batty Bat!'

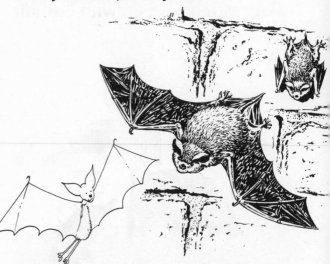

Timid Toad may simply be a COMMON TOAD

The Common Toad is an earthy colour, which is good camouflage for the toad likes to squat on damp soil and you could pass close by and miss seeing it completely. More important still, a Hissing Sid type snake might miss it too. The toad scoops out a little hollow for itself under a root which it makes its 'home' — and although it may leave on short hunting expeditions, it always goes back to base camp.

Artful Owl is a TAWNY OWL

Tawny Owls usually sleep in holes in trees or ruins. It may even take over the old nest of a crow and lay its round white eggs there. The most remarkable feature of the Tawny Owl is its ability to turn its head in almost a full circle. This is so it can keep its eye on an animal or object whilst flying around it. It's not certain why Owls are considered 'wise', but Artful Owl can genuinely be called wise for teaming up with Captain Beaky.

Reckless Rat could be a BROWN RAT

Rats originally came from Asia and made the adventurous journey across the high seas by stowing away in grain ships many decades ago. They climbed aboard by walking along mooring ropes and so avoided getting their feet wet. A rat, whether black or brown, will eat virtually anything and it is found wherever man has established himself. Rats can climb into attics to get food, and some have reputedly grown their fur long so as to live in food refrigerators! They are so versatile that it shouldn't surprise anyone to see a rat with a hat, and with a lasso for a tail — just like old Reckless Rat!

49

Spot Captain Beaky and His Friends

Hissing Sid is searching high and low for Captain Beaky and his brave band — Timid Toad, Reckless Rat, Artful Owl and Batty Bat. Can you spot where they're all hiding?

Blanche was a baby owl. And she was so keen to fly that she couldn't even wait till her feathers grew before she jumped off a branch into mid-air.

Now every bird needs feathers if it is to fly, and Blanche was no exception. So when she jumped off the branch she nose-dived to the ground before she could even blink.

Of course her mother was there to comfort her and lend her a wing to cry on. But Blanche was confused and said: ''Mother, I thought owls were supposed to be wise birds?''

''They are my dear,'' reassured her mother.

''Then how could I do such an unwise thing like fly without feathers?'' asked Blanche tearfully.

''Well,'' replied her mother. ''That's because, for owls — feathers and wisdom grow together.''

Puzzle Time

1. "Which is heavier?" asked Captain Beaky, "an ounce of gold or an ounce of feathers?"   "An ounce of gold, of course," answered Artful Owl. "But a pound of feathers is heavier than a pound of gold," he added.
Was Artful Owl right?

2. Timid Toad fell into a well 30 feet deep. He climbed up 3 feet every day and slipped back 2 feet every night. How long before Timid Toad reached the top?

3. In an orchard near where Captain Beaky lives, there are only apple trees, pear trees and cherry trees. One-third of the whole orchard are apple trees, one-fourth are pear trees, and there are 30 cherry trees.
How many trees does the orchard contain?   (Answers at the bottom of the page)

THREE TONGUE-TWISTERS FOR YOU TO TRY . . . .

> She sells sea-shells on the sea shore;
> The shells she sells are sea-shells I'm sure.
> So if she sells sea-shells on the sea shore,
> Then I'm sure she sells sea-shore shells.

REPEAT THIS TWISTER SIX TIMES QUICKLY — WITHOUT MIXING UP THE WORDS!
Six sheaves of sifted thistles,
Six sheaves of unsifted thistles,
And six thistle sifters.

How much wood would a woodchuck chuck — if a woodchuck could chuck wood? If a woodchuck could chuck wood, the wood that a woodchuck would chuck is the wood that a woodchuck could chuck, if the woodchuck that could chuck wood would chuck, or a woodchuck could chuck wood.

Answers to Puzzle Time

1), Yes! Artful Owl was right. Feathers are weighed by avoirdupois weight and gold by troy weight. An ounce troy has 480 grains, but an ounce avoirdupois has only 437½ grains.
On the other hand, a pound troy has only 12 ounces or 5760 grains, while a pound avoirdupois has 16 ounces or 7000 grains, so that an ounce of gold is heavier than an ounce of feathers, but a pound of gold is lighter than a pound of feathers.

2), On the 27th day, Timid Toad would have reached 29 feet before slipping back to 27 feet. So on the 28th day Timid Toad would have reached 30 feet, and as that is the top of the well he wouldn't slip back. So it took him 28 days.

3), One-third and one-fourth, when added together make seven-twelfths.
That means five-twelfths of the trees were cherry trees, of which there were thirty. One-twelfth of the trees would be six. Five-twelfths would be thirty, and twelve-twelfths of the total number of trees would be 12 x 6 = 72 trees.

52

How To Make Artful Owl

In fur fabric cut a 10cm diameter circle for body. Run a strong gathering thread round edge and stuff firmly with kapok or cut up nylons and as you pull up the gathers fasten off tightly.

For the head use an 8cm circle and make as for body. Place head on body — gathered edges together and ladder stitch firmly.

Cut out two white circles and two black circles for eyes. Two wings in fawn felt, two ears in fawn felt and two feet. Stick in position. Tie a bow of bright ribbon round his neck if you like.

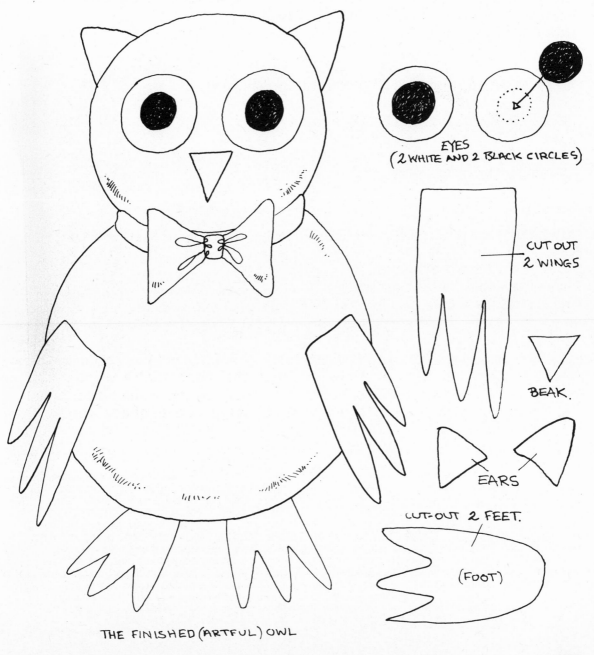

EYES
(2 WHITE AND 2 BLACK CIRCLES)

CUT OUT 2 WINGS

BEAK.

EARS

CUT-OUT 2 FEET.

(FOOT)

THE FINISHED (ARTFUL) OWL

Hissing Sid's Ambush

Captain Beaky was sunning himself near his home by the lake when ...

"'Ello," said a voice from the reeds. "'Ello . . . Can you 'ear me?"

"Am I hearing things?" muttered Captain Beaky to himself. "I could have sworn that was the voice of a French mouse."

"Quite right, monsieur," said the little mouse. "I am the ghost of a penniless French mouse called Jacques. I come 'ere to warn you about le snake you call — how you say — 'Issing Sid?"

"Yes," said Captain Beaky, taking deep breaths to calm his nerves. "I've just been thinking about old Sid. What's he been up to now, Jacques?"

"'E 'as — 'ow you say — 'atched a plot."

"What kind of plot, Jacques?"

"Mon Dieu! A nasty plot le snake 'atch!"

"Yes, yes," said the Captain. "You've said that. But can you be more specific. I mean what exactly does he intend to do?"

"Ambush, monsieur. He intends to ambush Capitaine Beaky and his merry Band. So take 'eed, monsieur."

The thin voice of the French mouse began to waver and then faded away and before the Captain knew where he was, the ghost of Jacques the French mouse also disappeared into thin air.

"I don't like this," muttered Captain Beaky, getting up and stretching himself. "I don't like this one little bit . . . . Why should a mousy French fellow pop out of nowhere to warn me of a mysterious plot against me and the gang. I think I'd better see what Batty Bat and Reckless Rat and Timid Toad and Artful Owl have to say about it all."

So the Captain gave a secret whistle and the woodland creatures passed it on until it reached the ears of his gang.

"What's it all about?" asked Batty Bat, zipping around the gang in great excitement.

"Ambush!" declared the Captain. "Hissing Sid wants to ambush us."

"But how can one feeble-minded, beady-eyed snake ambush a whole band of brave stout-hearted warriors like us?" asked Timid Toad, thrusting out his chest defiantly.

"You tell us!" squeaked Reckless Rat. "Because we can't figure it out either."

"What we need," cut in Captain Beaky, "is a spy in the enemy camp. That way we can find out what Sid intends to do, and then make plans to ambush *him* instead."

"Then it's got to be me," volunteered Artful Owl. "I'll hide in the oak tree and Hissing Sid will never know that two beady eyes are watching him from above."

Meanwhile, at the base of the old oak tree, two shifty eyes were gazing out into the undergrowth. These shifty eyes belonged to the snake with the shiftiest eyes in all Snakedom — the one and only Hissing Sid.

The base of the oak tree was Sid's home, and he had a guest in for lunch. Sid's guest also had shifty eyes, but it wasn't a snake ... it was a fox.

Sid and the fox had been discussing the weather, and about the price of partridge eggs, and had also been agreeing how they were both sick and tired of hearing

about Captain Beaky and his Band who were supposed to be the bravest animals in the land.

"They wouldn't be so brave if I caught them down a biggish rabbit hole," said Fox with a cat-like grin.

"How do you mean?" hissed Sid, egging him on. "What would you do to them if you caught them?"

"Eat them all alive!" snapped Fox. "That's what I'd do!"

"But you'd leave the left-overs for me, wouldn't you?" pleaded Sidney.

"Maybe, maybe not," shrugged Fox.

"But," said Sid, with an evil glint in his beady eye, "what if I were to lead them into a trap — an ambush where *you* would be waiting?"

Fox showed all his teeth as he grinned. "How would you arrange this little ambush, Sid?"

Sid writhed with excitement. "Listen carefully, Fox. It's like this, you see . . ."

Captain Beaky and his brave band were all snoozing under the shade of a big lime tree, and when the sun rolled a little further through the arc of heaven, Artful Owl flapped lazily into the air and flew towards them.

"Welcome back, Artful Owl," said Captain Beaky. "Now come and tell your story."

"Well this is what I heard from inside Sid's oak tree hide-out," began Artful Owl. "There's a big rabbit hole near the east side of the lake where a fox will hide tomorrow morning. Meanwhile, Sid intends to steal the handkerchief sail from our boat *HMS Most Leaky* and get us to chase him. He will then lead us into the rabbit hole where the fox will gobble us all up . . . leaving a few morsels for Sid to finish off. Then that will be the end of us . . . and . . . and no more songs will we sing and no more cruises in *HMS Most Leaky* . . ." At this point Artful Owl broke down and just stared at them all.

"Don't worry yourself, Artful Owl," soothed Captain Beaky. "If the worst comes to the worst we don't *have* to follow Sid, even if he does steal the mainsail from *HMS Most Leaky*. But, no! I think I've got an idea which should end up with this fox getting his ears boxed and Sid getting his slimy tail chewed off. This is what we'll do..."

That night, Batty Bat zipped along to see a friend of his who just happened to be a Badger. He told the Badger that he'd seen a big disused rabbit hole near the east side of the lake which would be ideal for a Badger set.

The Badger thanked Batty Bat for his information and said he'd move in immediately as he'd always wanted to have a home near the side of the lake. Then Batty Bat warned the Badger that a certain fox also wanted to move into the old rabbit hole, as did a beady-eyed snake.

The Badger chortled, "Foxes don't worry a Badger. I'll give it a clip around the ear and send it home with its tail between its legs. And as for snakes, why — I could eat them for breakfast!"

"Well, actually," piped Batty Bat. "This one is due a little later."

The Badger laughed. "Then I'll have him for lunch."

The following morning, as expected, Hissing Sid stole the sail from *HMS Most Leaky* and Captain Beaky and his brave band played the game; duly following at a safe distance.

Unsuspecting, Sid made straight for the big rabbit hole — stopping every so often to make sure that he was being followed. Luckily, Sid didn't see his friend the fox running in the *opposite* direction with a bent tail and a black eye!

Hissing Sid squirmed confidently into the rabbit hole.

Seconds later there was a 'Hiss' of fear and Sid came hurtling out of the hole, pursued by a great lumbering Badger. In five huge strides the Badger had caught Sid in his huge jaws and it looked as if that was how the snake would end its days. But suddenly Sid did a strange thing . . . He shed his skin — literally jumping out of it and he managed to squirm away into the thick grass wearing only his underclothes.

Afterwards, Captain Beaky and his gang went home and had a picnic; and it was a long time before Hissing Sid turned his mind to ambushes again . . . he was growing a new coat among other things.

The thing Desmond Duckling saw when he first opened his eyes was a fox! The egg he was living in opened with a crack when it was being stolen by a fox. (Foxes love the taste of ducks' eggs). And for a while Desmond thought the fox was his mother!

Most foxes would have eaten him, but luckily for Desmond, this particular fox had pity on the helpless baby duckling and took it back to its nest by the waterside.

The effect of this early meeting with a fox gave Desmond lots of courage — because when he grew up into a medium-sized duck he was always happy to pass the time of day with a fox. All the other ducks would be scuttling, paddling or flying for their lives, while Desmond would calmly quack, 'Good Day!' to the fox and carry on as if nothing had happened. And the foxes were so surprised by this that they had great respect for Desmond and left him in peace.

Dot to Dot

Join each group of dots to see some of your favourite characters.

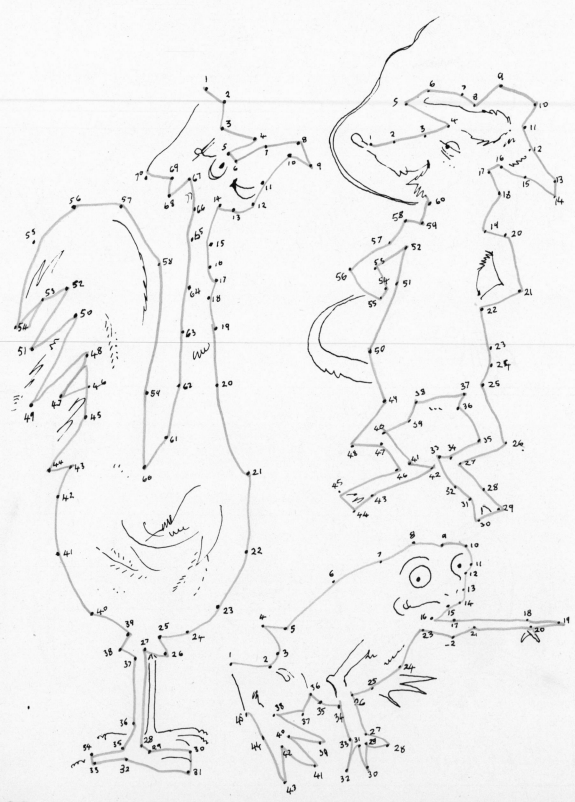

Spot the difference

Artful Owl and Timid Toad are discussing ways to capture Hissing Sid.
Can you spot the 10 differences between the two pictures?